P9-EKJ-059

CALGARY PUBLIC LIBRARY

SEP - 2012

Señorita Gordita

Helen Ketteman

Illustrated by
Will Terry

Albert Whitman & Company, Chicago, Illinois

Welcome new babies Hayley, Charlotte, Emily, and Meghan.—H.K.

For Myles.—W.T.

Library of Congress Cataloging-in-Publication Data
Ketteman, Helen.
Senorita Gordita / by Helen Ketteman ; illustrated by Will Terry.
p. cm.
Summary: Resets the tale of the Gingerbread boy in the southwest, where
the scrumptious Gordita eludes her pursuers until she meets a clever owl.
Includes glossary of Spanish terms and a gorditas recipe.
ISBN 978-0-8075-7302-0
[1. Fairy tales. 2. Folklore.] I. Terry, Will, 1966- ill.
II. Gingerbread boy. III. Title.
PZ8.K474Sen 2012 398.2—dc22 [E]2011008569

Text copyright © 2012 by Helen Ketteman.
Illustrations copyright © 2012 by Will Terry.
Published in 2012 by Albert Whitman & Company.
All rights reserved. No part of this book may be reproduced or transmitted in any form or by any means,
electronic or mechanical, including photocopying, recording, or by any information storage and
retrieval system, without permission in writing from the publisher.
Printed in the United States
10 9 8 7 6 5 4 3 2 1 LB 16 15 14 13 12 11

The design is by Carol Gildar.

For more information about Albert Whitman & Company,
visit our web site at www.albertwhitman.com.

Araña wiggled her legs as she set the gordita on a paper towel to drain. "You're one tasty-looking gordita! I'm in for a treat."

But that gordita hopped up. "Oh no, Araña! I'm one fast gordita! You can't catch me!" And with a flip and a skip and a zip-zoom-zip, the gordita raced out the door.

"Señorita Gordita! Come back!" called Araña, chasing after her.

But Señorita Gordita zipped through the desert till she came to a creosote bush. Lagarto was resting underneath. He opened one eye.

"Hola, Señorita Gordita! Come share my shade," he said.
"You look delicious . . . I mean, hot."

Señorita Gordita jumped aside. "Oh no, amigo! I ran from Araña so fast, I left her spinning. I'll run away from you, too. I'm putting the pedal to the metal. Adiós, Lagarto!"

And with a flip and a skip and a zip-zoom-zip, off she ran. Lagarto skittered after her.

Señorita Gordita sped along until she came to an arroyo.
Crótolo slithered up.

"Buenos días, Señorita Gordita. S-s-say,
you s-s-smell s-s-scrumptious. Come visit awhile."

"Buenos días, Crótolo, but no thanks. I airstreamed
Araña and gassed past Lagarto. So keep your fangs to
yourself, Crótolo!"

And with a flip and a skip and a zip-zoom-zip, off she ran. Crótolo slithered after her.

After a while, she stopped to rest on the limb of a mesquite tree. Escorpión curled his stinger over his back.

"Hola Señorita Gordita! You look tasty . . . I mean, lovely. Come a little closer, amiga," he said.

"I am rather fine-looking, aren't I? But I airstreamed Araña, gassed past Lagarto, and cruised past Crótolo. So put down your zinger of a stinger, Escorpión. You'll never catch me!"

And with a flip and a skip and a zip-zoom-zip, she left Escorpión in a cloud of dust. Escorpión joined the chase.

Señorita Gordita ran on. After a while, she came upon Javalina, who was munching on a prickly pear cactus.

Javalina snorted. "Hola, amiga! Why the rush? Come join me for a lunch munch."

Señorita Gordita shook her head. "No way, Javalina! You might want to lunch-munch me! But I airstreamed Araña, gassed past Lagarto, cruised past Crótolo, and dusted Escorpión. And I'll lose you too, amigo."

And with a flip and a skip and a zip-zoom-zip,
she hustled away. Javalina joined the chase.

Señorita Gordita laughed. "I'm zip-zoom fast as fast can be! No desert beast will lunch on me!" Soon, she came upon Coyote scratching at a ground squirrel burrow.

"Buenos días, Señorita Gordita! Come help me dig out this burrow. There's a fat ground squirrel inside. Enough for both of us."

"No, Señor Coyote! You look hungry, amigo. I airstreamed Araña, gassed past Lagarto, cruised past Crótolo, dusted Escorpión, and hustled away from Javalina. And I'll ditch you, too!"

And with a flip and a skip and a zip-zoom-zip, Señorita Gordita sped away. Coyote chased behind.

Señorita Gordita laughed. "I love to run. It's fun, fun, fun!" She whizzed along until she came to a tall saguaro, reaching its giant arms up to the sky.

"Who-o-o goes there?" asked Búho.
"Me! Señorita Gordita."

Búho blinked his big yellow eyes. "I see a cloud of dust is coming. Are you being chased?"

"Yes! But I'm zip-zoom fast. No one can catch me!"

"They could if you get too tired," said Búho. "Jump up here where you can rest safely for a bit."

Señorita Gordita cocked her head.
"That cloud of dust is a group of critters
who want to eat me. Maybe that's what
you want."

"Who-o-o, me?" asked Búho. "I hunt and eat at night. As you can see, it's daytime. The dust cloud is getting closer. You'd best get moving, señorita."

Señorita Gordita looked at the approaching dust cloud. Búho was right. She did feel tired. And hot. A rest would be good. "Búho!" she shouted.

Búho blinked. "Yes?"

"Thanks for your offer. I'll come up for a rest."

Señorita Gordita took a huge leap and landed beside Búho high on the saguaro.

In an instant, Búho grabbed Señorita Gordita in his talons and opened his sharp beak. And soon, there was nothing left of Señorita Gordita except a few crumbs.

"Being zip-zoom-fast is good, señorita," said Búho. "But being smart is better."

Glossary

Gordita ....Gordita is a term of endearment meaning "little fat one" in Spanish. It also refers to a thick, fried tortilla made of masa harina (corn flour) and topped with various things. It's a favorite street vendor food in Mexico.

Adiós ....Goodbye

Amigo, Amiga ...Friend

Araña ....Spider

Buenos días ....Good day

Búho ....Owl

Crótolo ....Rattlesnake

Ecsorpión .....Scorpion

Hola ....Hello

Largarto ......Lizard

Señorita.......Miss

Señor .... Mister

Some words are the same in English and Spanish:

Saguaro ....Saguaro, a very tall cactus

Arroyo ....arroyo, a stream

Coyote ....coyote

Recipe for Gorditas
Makes 6 servings

1 cup masa harina (Masa harina is corn flour traditionally used to make corn tortillas. It can be found in the ethnic foods section of larger grocery stores.)

3/4 cups chicken broth

1/8 cup vegetable oil

1/4 cup plus 1-1/2 teaspoons all-purpose flour

1/4 teaspoon salt

1/2 teaspoon baking powder

Vegetable oil

Stir together masa harina and broth in a mixing bowl. Cover and let stand 30 minutes. Add shortening, flour, salt, and baking powder; beat at medium speed with an electric mixer until smooth.

Divide dough into 6 golf-sized balls. Arrange on wax paper, and cover with damp towels. Pat each ball of dough into a 3-inch circle. Pinch edges of circles to form a ridge, and press a well into each center with a spoon to hold toppings.

Let a grown-up do this part: Pour oil to a depth of 1/4 inch into a large skillet; over medium to high heat. Fry gorditas about two minutes on each side, or until golden brown. Drain on paper towels.

You can top the gorditas with refried beans, sour cream, salsa, and cilantro.